Little Raccoon
Learns to Share

ISBN 978-0-545-80223-9

12 11 10 9 8 7 6 5 4 3 2   16 17 18 19/0

Printed in the U.S.A.   40

First Scholastic printing, September 2014

Little Raccoon
Learns to Share

By Mary Packard
Illustrated by Lisa McCue

SCHOLASTIC INC.

Little Raccoon's favorite word was "Mine!"

She liked to keep her things nice and clean. She wanted
them right near her, just in case she needed them.

What's more, Little Raccoon liked to be
first. That way she didn't have to take turns . . .

. . . and she would always be sure to get the most.

One day Little Raccoon decided to pick berries. When she saw her friends coming, she hid with her basket behind a bush.

If they eat my berries, she worried,
there might not be enough for me!

Little Raccoon peeked through the bushes.
Little Beaver is catching lots of fish, she thought,
and everyone is having so much fun.

"I can't eat all these fish by myself," she heard Little Beaver say.
"Why don't you all come back to my house for a fish fry?"

"Okay," said Little Chipmunk. "I'll bring acorn stuffing."
"I'll bring biscuits and honey," Little Bear called down.
"And I'll make some applesauce," Little Wolf offered.

Little Raccoon wanted to go, too, but she didn't want to leave her berries.
Because her friends didn't see her, they didn't invite her to join them.

Little Raccoon walked home. She was glad that her basket was still full of berries. But somehow she was feeling more sad than glad.

Little Raccoon told her mother about the party.

"We could bake some muffins with your berries," suggested Mrs. Raccoon. "You could take them to the party and share them with your friends."

Little Raccoon wasn't so sure about the sharing part, but she did love to bake.

So she set aside a bowl of berries to eat later and used the rest in the muffins.

Little Raccoon couldn't decide what to do. Finally, she went to the party.

Standing on Little Beaver's doorstep, Little Raccoon could hear her friends laughing inside. *It sure would be fun to join them*, she thought.

But then a troubling idea popped into her head. *If everyone shares my muffins*, she worried, *there might not be enough for me!*

Just then, Little Beaver came to the door. "Little Raccoon!" he exclaimed. "Come in and join the party. How nice that you brought muffins!" he said.

Little Beaver took the muffins from her. Little Raccoon didn't know what to do.

Then everyone came to welcome her. Pretty soon, Little Raccoon
was having so much fun, she forgot all about her muffins.

Little Raccoon shared her tools with Little Bear,
who had good ideas about what to build.

Later, Little Bear returned the tools still
good as new and gave Little Raccoon
one of the toy boats she built.

That day, Little Raccoon discovered that sharing with others wasn't so bad after all. And she found out something else, too. When you share with others, they share with you!